ALSO BY SIMON VAN BOOY

FICTION

The Secret Lives of People in Love: Stories
Love Begins in Winter: Stories
Everything Beautiful Began After
The Illusion of Separateness
Tales of Accidental Genius: Stories
Father's Day
The Sadness of Beautiful Things: Stories
Night Came with Many Stars

NONFICTION

Why We Need Love
Why Our Decisions Don't Matter
Why We Fight

CHILDREN'S FICTION

Gertie Milk & the Keeper of Lost Things
Gertie Milk & the Great Keeper Rescue

THE PRESENCE OF ABSENCE

The Presence
of Absence

A NOVEL

Simon Van Booy

Boston
GODINE
2022

Published in 2022 by
GODINE
Boston, Massachusetts

LIBRARY OF CONGRESS CATALOGING-IN-PUBLICATION DATA
Names: Van Booy, Simon, author.
Title: The presence of absence / Simon Van Booy.
Description: Boston : Godine, 2022.
Identifiers: LCCN 2022005078 (print) | LCCN 2022005079
    (ebook) | ISBN 9781567927443 (hardback)
    ISBN 9781567927450 (ebook)
Subjects: LCGFT: Novellas.
Classification: LCC PR6122.A36 P74 2022 (print) | LCC PR6122.A36
    (ebook) | DDC 823/.92--dc23/eng/20220207
LC record available at https://lccn.loc.gov/2022005078
LC ebook record available at https://lccn.loc.gov/2022005079

First Printing, 2022
Printed in the United States of America

Always, for C.E.D.

Then love, love will tear us apart again . . .

Joy Division

Prologue

SOME YEARS AGO, I received a letter from a woman in New Jersey. She wanted to talk on the telephone regarding her late husband, the author Max Little. I had attended the odd reading of Little's over the years and had four of his books on the shelf at home—one of which he signed for me in San Francisco at the beginning of 2007, when we chatted briefly about the absence of tea kettles in American hotel rooms (Max was also British).

After talking with Hadley Little for two hours one Sunday afternoon, it came to light that her husband had left a small journal of his last days, and Hadley wanted to see it published posthumously. Max Little's book editor Carrie K. at Sipsworth House had already examined the work and felt it too fragmented in its original form and not indicative of the whole story, which continues to this day. Eventually it was decided that Hadley would approach me with the idea of incorporating the fragments of her husband's final thoughts into a novel that I would write and publish under my own name with an introduction explaining the circumstances of our collaboration.

Shortly after our conversation, a package arrived from Sipsworth House with a copy of the manuscript. As I started reading, it was soon very clear that Max Little had intended his thoughts to be shared, despite the intensely personal nature of this work. But the book wasn't much more than a short collection of notes, with no dates to indicate any intended order. Despite the challenges, I found that I was soon emotionally attached to the work, and agreed with Hadley and her late husband's editorial team that the only way to convey the story in the way Little may have intended was to incorporate the dying author's feelings and observations into something with structure. Like many authors I know, I believe that a story will often choose a particular writer to bring it into the world, by some mysterious process that is both instinctual and deliberate. This is why a work of fiction seemed like the best way forward.

It's an unexpectedly intimate experience getting to know someone after they have died. If such a thing is even possible, then language really does have magical qualities. I am honored by the trust Hadley and all at Sipsworth House placed in me, and grateful for the friendship that has developed as a result. At Hadley's request, all the names in the book have been altered to protect the privacy of herself and others. This includes her husband's, which was changed to Max Little, so if you type his name into the internet you'll discover some interesting people, but none connected to this work. I have tried to remain true to Little's evolving vision of life and death throughout the text, but should you find any weak areas, they are most assuredly a result of my hand, while any parts you find worthy of praise will undoubtedly be the work of Little.

—Simon Van Booy

THE PRESENCE OF ABSENCE

PART ONE

IN VIVO

27.

MOST READERS EXPECT some crisis in a story's first pages. The idea being that if you keep reading, the narrator has succeeded in distracting you long enough to forget you exist outside the book, where—like me—you are dying.

All I have this time is my life. Or what's left of it.

The square hospital room from which I type this missive is as familiar to me now as my own hands. There are two windows, one in the door and another in the wall, but I have not been outside for almost eight months. In that time, however, I have visited places and people as permitted by the drunk librarian of memory, whose random dispatches have not led back into the past, but into the future where there is often clarity—but also helplessness.

And so if contrived disaster *is* why you're here—to be diluted by the suffering of others—then I suggest you stop reading and put this book down. Find a parable-style work with a cover that has been purposefully designed to trick you. I mean it. I'm not joking, nor am I trying to be antisocial. I won't tell you what this story is about, and you can just go on with your life—forget the moment ever happened—never think of me again as you step back from the unexpected intimacy.

In this story, pain is the only reliable proof of happiness.

26.

You do realize that by turning the page you've decided to follow a complete stranger down a possibly meaningless path?

I'm going to try and lead you home by a different road. Home is where you've been wanting to go for some time. It's why you read; unless you're in school and this is forced, in which case, you have my sympathies, as childhood is a series of small disasters that conspire to become something precious.

If this story doesn't get you all the way home, you'll at least feel closer. I know because there's already a bond between us. If I didn't sense it right now, I would stop all this.

I've arrived here after reading books and authoring books, some of which you may have suffered through in the past. The point is, I know enough now to recognize that everything I've written was child's play—actually, not as wise, because children know they're playing. Whereas we deceive ourselves into believing play is real, while the truth slips further and further away, until one day rearing up, perhaps after an ordeal, disguised as a terrifying monster we once tried to assimilate as a god—something that has come from outside to obliterate, but in reality, has risen from within.

25.

IT'S TIME TO begin our journey forward by moving through what is past. Our destination lies on the other side, though is yet to be imagined. We will get there together, and there will be others, but you will not know the others.

Through the *act* of reading this novel, it's actually *you* telling the story. For example, when you see words, what's imagined comes from your experience of life, not mine:

The bus appeared at twilight

We were almost home when rain turned to snow

In the afternoon we simply walked, arm in arm across the cold sand

He was sleeping, when

That was our first kiss, then, in

How could I know the things you've seen and felt in the years we've been apart?

This journey won't feel like remembering—more like a dream, because I control the structure of what you see, but never the content. That's for you to feast upon.

What are you imagining?

Feast takes *me* to Romans in togas at long tables. A mosaic pieced together by small fingers I cannot see but know were there. It's June and I'm a sweating child in shorts. Thirsty. At Chester Museum on a school trip in nineteen-eighty-something. Just standing there, staring at the ancient multitude, overcome with despair at not having enough money to buy a toy centurion in the gift shop. I've eaten my lunch but feel hungry again. I'm also wondering where *she* is. I didn't see her on the school bus, or in the chattering queue that snaked all the way back to Ancient Egypt.

All that from the word *feast*.

Where did *you* go? We started in the same vicinity but saw and felt different things. Stories lead us behind the curtain of somebody else's life into the deepest chambers of our own. And so, the events that take place in this narrative have already happened to you. This book is your past but also your future.

What a relief it's only *your* voice that can be heard as you crawl headfirst through tunnels of sentence. Emotion comes from your relationship to the words themselves, and the words in relation to other words. There is less of me here than you think. Maybe none. Maybe only a ghost hovering between each silent resurrection.

And though we may never be together in body, this book will ensure that we never part. That you and I, in this moment, are the universe in soft and difficult pieces.

24.

THIS STORY IS mostly about *her*. The *she* I mentioned. My life partner.

(Who will you cast in the role?)

She is out there now, in the world. You might see her and never know. She's walking around. Listen for her shoes on the concrete if you live in a city. Watch for the orange flash of her turn signal on a crowded highway. She was driving a white car the last time I saw her. And every Wednesday at a club she plays tennis, which to me has always seemed like a game of punctuation with the net as a sentence neither player dares to conclude. But, god almighty, she was good. Such a powerful serve.

Grace and form on the return, too. She had it all. Unbelievable.

And she's out there now over the top of this book, dancing without music like everyone else. She's hair and teeth and painted lips sipping wine and laughing through the restaurant window.

To you, just some woman.

A face that moves.

A body that turns by itself.

But to me.

Life doesn't start when you're born—it begins when you commit yourself to the eventual devastating loss that results from connecting to a person who to everyone else appears completely ordinary. This story is woven from the fabric of my devotion to someone who could be anyone to you, which is why you should cast your own hero.

Sex doesn't matter.

Gender doesn't matter.

Age and physical appearance don't matter.

It's in the eyes. That's where you can tell. And, of course, by how—long after they've disappeared from your life—you somehow find a way to go on.

Loving them.

23.

You might be wondering where I am, where this voice is coming to you from—even though there's no sound and it's *your* voice you can hear. Perhaps you would like to know which hospital? The town? If I'm still around, and if not, how many years have elapsed since?

None of that matters, because our lives are braided *here* and *now* by this sentence.

Most books lie about all that. Questioning the voice is not rewarded. But I'm tired of the deceit, even by omission or by habit—which is why, before I hand over the reins of this story to you, I need to point out that every person is, at the very least, two people simultaneously.

The first split occurs in childhood, the moment you say something that is not truly how you feel. From that point forward, you have a *second voice* to negotiate your way through the world, while the *first voice* retreats. This is the person I hope I've been speaking to: the one behind the curtain. Remember that here, in this place, we're not obliged to defer intimacy. Trust is immediate. In this book, duplicity is acknowledged. Here, small but determined waves of language move between our shores.

So, will you run with me in the wilderness, side by side, like the animals we once were and will be again?

Sorry.

Sometimes I get carried away by sudden gusts of feeling. Especially now, in this cool, hard bed, I can move up and down with a button, like some navigational instrument as we row through the dark toward morning.

By the way, I'm not the first person to point out a duplicity of the self, the idea of a *first* and *second voice*. It's everywhere in art: a mirror in which you see a version of yourself that's been hiding.

Remember Ibsen's *A Doll's House*? Specifically at the end of the play, that moment Nora reverts to *first voice* and her world ends. She must now separate from Nora's husband, separate from Nora's children. Untangle herself from the memories of a woman she has been impersonating.

Are you familiar with Cordelia, the youngest and most favored daughter in Shakespeare's *King Lear*? Cordelia tries to share *first voice* with her father and gets banished for it—but not from herself . . . only from what she could never be.

So, if the voice most of us share with the world is not the inner voice, *the first voice,* then all our adult relationships inevitably begin with deceit.

Even the ones that don't end that way.

Anyway, we must get on. I have to stay focused. The notion of a *third voice* will come later. From this point, what time I have left will be spent cultivating what's left of yours.

22.

BASED ON MY current situation here in bed, I've learned that it's best to sincerely pretend to not know who you are, nor where you are. Then anything you figure out must be true, as it's not from assumption, but direct, immediate experience of the moment.

You might be reading this book on the train to Gare du Nord; soaked to the skin in a jungle; sailing up some caramel river at dawn; in a Beijing hotel with the curtains drawn at midday; or at home in a chair as evening opens like a dark flower.

Maybe you are close to the moon on a vessel of sleepers in the breath of space, one stitch in the jeweled cloth—those dead eyes of a living god.

Perhaps you are, like me, prostrate in a hospital bed.

Anyway, stop reading this book and look around for a moment.

Go on.

I mean it. *Look around . . . now.*

(If someone notices you and also starts looking, you have my permission to laugh.)

Do you see?

While out there in the world with this book, you are also here, mummified by these sentences in a non-physical universe. The body and the mind can travel independently of each other. Perhaps one day they'll go so far as to be lost. I'm not saying it's bad, I'm just saying it's possible—and I, of all people, should know. For instance, I'm writing this in the present, and you're reading it in the present. Except there is a gulf of time between us.

I might even be dead.

Yet, here I am.

Between the page and your eye.

Countless paradoxes like this redeem language.

But the voice cleaved in two during childhood is not a paradox of language. It's a division of self, which is the multiplication of possibility. Don't worry. Again, I'm not saying it's bad. It might even ripen in us the appetite for love, the impulse to dab color onto stretched cotton, to make sounds that are beyond anything rational, but that sharpen rationality and make us see for the first time what we've been looking at our whole lives.

And so, as I said earlier, birth is a false start. It's in the country of childhood where our lives really get going—where the stage is set, the players readied, and the lines put down for everything that is happening to you right now.

21.

THERE WAS A television in the corner of my room in the early days. Before the pain was controlled, I used it as a tool to distract—though I'm not going to tell you anything about the treatments, nor what my *corpus* has been through, because feeling sorry for me is not why we're here, remember? I don't want this book to be a distraction from life, but a way for you to go deeper.

I've since had the television removed, but having it for a time did make me wonder how bad childhood was before soaps and action-drama. For thousands of years, without this glowing window into others' lives, children must have felt their home environments were completely normal. Now, parents can no longer indulge their delusions between the front and back doors.

As a boy in Wales, I wanted my life to be like *The A-Team*. I wanted it to be like *Knight Rider*. But it wasn't like *Knight Rider*. Nor was it like *Dallas* or *Falcon Crest*.

My life was walking to school worried my socks were too red. One morning, as I neared the grassy knoll before the busy road I had practiced crossing with my father over and over, I heard my name in the mouth of another boy. I turned and there he was, barreling toward me, lips curled back to reveal a mad riddle of teeth. It seemed he was cupping something precious in his loosely clenched fists, something he was determined to share with me. What was it? A butterfly wing? Pincers from a stag beetle? A 1970s soda can ring pull? World War II aircraft bullet casing? (Chris Page once found three by the BMX track along with a porno mag in the hedge.)

But then the red-faced boy was spitting words over bared incisors: *Paki! Wog! Paki bastard!*

I would hear these often growing up. They're woven into the fabric of my life, part of our story. I learned to fight but never refute their claim—for if it wasn't me, it would have been someone, some other small body, some other brown hand like mine that picked up toys and reached for the deep fur of any passing dog.

Those words were most certainly the red-faced boy's *second voice*. But I wonder if with *first voice,* he was saying: *Ilovemydad. Ihatemydad. Ilovemydad. Ihatemydad. Helovesme. Mumcriesallnightwiththebathroomdoorlocked. Hercriesdislodgemyinsides. Shelovesdad. Ilovemydad. Tohangon. Tolove. Imusthit. It'snormal. Hastobe. Willfindareason. Skin . . . Body . . . Voice. Anythingtosavemyselfandmum. Anddad. WhoIwillalwayshate. Loving.*

As I lie here in this hospital bed, old enough to think I'm not old, I'm starting to wonder if all hate isn't just the unbearable pain of inexpressible love.

I think the first blow landed in the middle of my forehead. Then I was on my back, his knuckle ramming, grinding my head bone and eye sockets. We were like a single machine in the act of breaking down.

Another digression: Try and imagine somebody at work has dragged you from your cubicle and is beating you next to the photocopy machine; blood runs down your chin; you can taste metal in your mouth; teeth wobble with any pressure from the tongue.

Everyone in the office is watching this—even people you like. Some are not just watching but laughing.

When the kicking stops, you lie there for a while, then drag your bruised, shamed body to the opaque glass doors of those in charge. They pretend to be upset and ask questions. They write things down.

After a while they come to believe *you* are somehow to blame for your own victimization.

You go home.

People you love act as though it were your fault, too.

You withdraw your heart from public circulation, like a library book no one can read without damaging.

Then, a week later, it happens again.

This time, others join in; it's the only way they can make sure it never happens to them.

You can't go to the police because your colleagues are, for some reason, immune to prosecution. And they know this. They can do anything they want to you.

You can't leave the office or get another job because you're not allowed to. The people in charge and the people you love are criminally obtuse. You simply must find a way to live with monumental shame and suffering, to let part of yourself die so that other parts may go on living.

This is what it means to be bullied.

When I opened my eyes, I was still on the ground. I couldn't see much because of wetness and swelling. But then something happened, the deus ex machina that makes this book possible. As the rock-hand was pounding the rubbery mass of my bloodied nose, from the sky came divine intervention in the form of a pink tennis racquet with rabbit stickers on the handle. It struck the boy only once, but with such force that in the following days, kids at school would say his cheek looked like fleshy graph paper.

I lay there for what seemed like all day but was probably one minute.

I was waiting for *her* to go away.

But she wouldn't go away.

She sat down, cross-legged, and pretended to pet the rabbit stickers on the frame of her pink tennis racquet, supposedly to make me laugh.

When I didn't move, she opened her lunch box and put a small package of very expensive cookies next to my cheek. But I just lay there on the grass, mesmerized by pain and the very expensive cookies, hoping she would think I was dead and bugger off.

But she didn't bugger off. She tried to help me up, which was intensely irritating. Then she trailed me to the school gates, and all the way into class where, thank god, she went to the place she usually sat, as I went to mine.

Although she was the most annoying and thoroughly unbearable creature I had ever encountered, over the next few months I managed to finish countless poems about her, which I hid in the record sleeve of my favorite album, *Wham! Greatest Hits*. I also became an avid tennis fan. I imagined us as grownups in the crowd behind the players, wearing stonewashed jeans, terry-cloth socks, and Yves Saint Laurent sunglasses that came free with any purchase of fragrance.

But the truth is, I didn't speak to Hadley for several years after the incident with our bully—except to ask if she knew the capital of Copenhagen during a geography test.

The point is, she saved me, and this story is about how—more than two decades later—I had to save her.

20.

Before I tell you everything important, I need to think for a moment; dying has given me the luxury of time by taking it away.

So, it was an act of violence that brought Hadley and me together—a moment of fierceness and courage (and good aim) on her part, but cruelty nonetheless that began our friendship and led eventually to marriage.

After our move to New York, when the internet became part of our daily lives, I looked for the bully.

Nothing on MySpace.

Not a single thing anywhere.

Years later, I searched with Hadley—she remembered more about him—and this time we were on Facebook.

Zip. Zilch, not a sausage.

It turns out he didn't have a presence because he was dead, had ceased living before we allowed social media to preserve the moments of our lives by stealing them.

Eventually we discovered a single newspaper article about him through Google, a story someone had scanned in for reasons we will never know. At eighteen, he'd been tried and found guilty of assaulting his own child, her sixteen-year-old mother, and a police officer named Sebastian. At nineteen, he hung himself with a prison bedsheet.

From his short, violent existence had sprung everything in mine that is beautiful.

If there is such a thing as fate, it's not that life is already written and we're simply unwitting figures in lines of spiritual code—it's that we are at the mercy of things imposed on us in childhood. The future of humanity is not decided by politicians in big rooms with untouched glasses of water, but by children at recess untangling the world through play.

Furthermore, if it hadn't been for a drunk, who in 1981 lunged for my future-wife's-mother's-breasts in a pub because Manchester United beat Liverpool, which resulted in her smashing a pint glass over his head in front of her seven-year-old, tennis-obsessed daughter, then Hadley and I would be on different paths, two oblivious human comets, which we are anyway because perfection is not a singular propitious direction, but the mechanism of choice.

Okay, let's get on now.

You can't change the past, only look for clues in a puzzle in which looking for clues is a clue.

19.

I'M AWAKE IN my hospital bed. All the lights are off. It is dawn and the sky is a faint canvas upon which the day will be sketched. I hear someone—probably the night nurse—going back and forth outside my door. Her shoes make dry squeaks like a thirsty mouse.

Oh, wait.

A light has just come on.

The glass in my door has warmed from gray to gentle orange. There is no lock or handle, just a small window with wire mesh between squares of glass. Once, I caught Hadley staring in through the grid, as though our lives' problems were something to be solved by mathematics. I pretended not to see. She was there for a long time looking in. When Hadley finally entered, I was going to make a joke about what she was doing, but then she kissed me and her cheek was wet so I decided not to play games.

A trolley just rolled past my room at speed, which is curious because it's too early for breakfast.

Nothing about today has been decided; the sun has yet to relieve her anemic sister.

I'm going to keep the light off as long as I can.

There's a button near my pillow—not the one that makes the bed go up and down, but for a lamp that I never put on because it's dazzling, though useful, I suppose, for people with failing sight.

My window to *out there*—where you are now—is not the seething black it was when I started typing today. Night is draining. I feel good about that. And about *this*: us being together. Good company you are.

I haven't seen Hadley or Jeremy for a few days now. That's a long time in my world. But they've been traveling. I told them to, insisted really, that they get some time away from the hospital—I even offered to pay for it, told Hadley to max out my credit card, which made them both laugh.

Jeremy said he found some foreign editions of my books for sale at the Strand, not the big ones I'm known for as a novelist, but the slimmer works—novellas and short stories. He thought they might look nice on the small shelf here in my room, beside the pile of magazines Hadley adds to with each visit.

There was a time I believed it was me writing the words in those books; that was before I understood that I could very well have been you.

Don't fret. This isn't going to be a work like those others I've made. I will never actually see this one the way you see it, feel it as you feel it in your hands—which is okay, as it's more a prayer of gratitude to nothing for everything.

At least that's how I feel now: finally happy enough to give up memory for good. Not that I have a choice when it comes to what I retain and what I relinquish. Some of the treatments have been difficult. Not the pain so much as the sickness after, but as I mentioned, that's not really relevant to this story.

So.

Here we are.

In dawn's path.

I can't hear birds yet.

The sky is just a weak glow with a few purple cheeks.

Hadley usually stays late enough for me to fall asleep. I'm looking forward to the possibility. In the early days, she would stay all night, lying next to me on the bed, atop the sheets. The night nurse didn't mind.

When Jeremy stayed, he would sleep upright in a chair with a hospital blanket, though by morning it usually lay in a soft mound at his feet, which were usually turned inward, giving him the air of a child.

Hadley and Jeremy are quite used to me being in this place, and both are ready for what is going to happen.

I'm ready, too. Everything has been talked through. Life will go on, just not for me.

If I don't see another dawn, it's because I am a part of it.

Look for me there.

18.

EVERYTHING I'VE TOLD you so far, while being the truth of what I can remember, is also a fiction, as past events can only be recollected in the room of the present. I'm different now from the person I was when the event took place, and so it's possible I am recalling details more pertinent to my current self, which thereby invalidates the memory. Alternatively, I might be remembering events in the context of how I felt then, which does not reflect my current state.

And so there's always tension. Selves that cannot be reconciled—except perhaps through the absence of memory in meditation or prayer.

You wouldn't believe the dreams I have here. Some-times they help me understand things. The worst one was perhaps the most helpful. In the dream, I died and found myself in a tearoom with people I knew decades ago. They all looked as I remembered them and spoke as if no time had passed between us. Was this some version of heaven? The land of milk and two sugars? I was dead but conscious and comfortable.

Since becoming ill, I have often felt sad that my physical death would be accompanied by the com-plete loss of memory. All the precious things I had experienced would cease to exist. To think, all those places and people who had brought me such deep joy, gone forever.

Anyway, in the dream, sipping tea with Andy the Hippy, Jim, Tanya, Sean, Rod, and Ken Gale, I asked how I might reach my wife, who was still down there living her life. Perhaps there was some window through which I could watch things going on, moment by moment?

Oh, there was nothing like that, they told me. Our lot was to remain in the tearoom for an indefinite amount of time. There was no way back to the world. I would never see my wife again and never know what happened to her after I died. Furthermore, her tearoom would be different.

That was it.

We'd had our time.

On waking, I lay still in the bed, blinking my eyes, floating in the wake of this nightmare and grateful to be back in the hospital room, which is something I hadn't felt before. Hell, I realized then, was to be fully conscious after death with memory intact.

And yet the retention of memory beyond physical death is something people seem to wish for, and seek to achieve through the worship of gods that exist always outside of us—separate and silent, a raging sea we cannot enter.

No longer afraid of losing my memory—wishing for it, even—I began to wonder if there wasn't some part of me that existed beyond memory, that was neither rooted in appetite and corporeal, nor an empirical self contrived over decades, arbitrarily, as a response to environment.

Imagine some part of my being that I could potentially go through my whole life without ever realizing was there.

It was quite soon after being diagnosed that I received the gift of this deeper awareness, the existence of something beyond self.

Let's go back and I'll tell you about it.

17.

WHEN I FIRST found out I was sick, two years ago, I didn't know what to do. I couldn't tell my wife, for reasons I'll go into later. The doctor said I had some time before the illness would start to show. A year, she said, maybe more depending on various things.

But the diagnosis was final. There was no hope for a cure.

Why should I be surprised? People die all the time. It's what we do. Yet, I suppose I never thought it would actually happen to me. Or is it that I didn't know *when* it would happen, or that I believed it would be so quick I wouldn't realize I was dead, or perhaps so painful the release would be a final mercy?

When I left the doctor's office on Lexington Avenue, I was shaking. I felt unsteady, as though I were walking on sponges. I couldn't believe how people were just ambling along looking at their phones as though everything was as it had been when I first woke up that morning. Later, I realized that everyone was acting normally because, like me before, they felt wholeheartedly that they were not dying.

When I arrived home from the clinic, I dropped my keys in the Wedgwood bowl. It sounded the same, the clatter of metal on porcelain, yet everything was different. They were no longer the same keys and it was another dish reconstructed from my memory of the one I had seen that morning. It felt like a different apartment, too, one I was visiting for the first time, but based on one I had lived in before.

Traumatic events can make you a stranger in your own life.

I wanted to cry fiercely then, wring the shock from my body so I might begin to think clearly. But I couldn't. It was because I didn't believe it yet.

So, I fed the plants with a copper watering can my wife and I bought in Paris after I published my first short story in a small but relevant magazine. The handle felt cold in my hand. Was that normal? Would it have felt so cold if I wasn't dying? Was I sick on top of being terminally ill?

Ironically, the watering can came from a taxidermy shop on Rue du Bac that also sells gardening supplies. Had I known at the time of purchase that such an item would be used on the day I was diagnosed with terminal illness, I might have woken up a bit then.

After the plants were taken care of, I just went about the apartment, looking at things. Do people ever walk around their homes, wondering which room they will die in? Whether it will be a Wednesday night or Saturday morning at the table with toast and coffee.

What would happen to things like knives and forks once I was gone. Would my wife keep them? Or would they be given away and used to fill other hungry mouths? Perhaps, along with my record collection, they were destined for a gigantic hole in the ground, where they would sit for thousands of years in compacted darkness, until excavated by robots trying to recoup resources for humans vacating the planet.

I didn't think about all this back then though, silverware and death and robots going through garbage. I just made toast and ate standing by the window, watching workmen walk around a small hole they had made while I was out at the clinic. When one of them looked up, I waved. He waved back, but his heart wasn't in it.

And the books I had written, clustered in a corner of the bookcase, now seemed inextricably linked to exile and sadness. Not *my* sadness, of course, but one that was coming for Hadley. Those books I had authored, peppered with people and places she knew, would become symbols of what she had lost—though, in truth, they were exactly the opposite.

But grief is a frantic, inconsolable child.

After toast, I boiled water. Then switched on the television, but not for long. The voices, the untenable certainty of prerecording, made me suddenly afraid.

I brewed tea and squeezed in honey from a plastic bear.

I sifted mail.

There was nothing else to do that didn't lead me off a thought-cliff.

So I had a bath and tried to read a book about what animals feel. But it was hard to concentrate because while sitting in the warm water, I realized I was impersonating myself, pretending to be the man I had been before I found out.

Yet I *was* that same man, naked in the bath, with

the same head, same hands, same ridiculous penis. Nothing had truly changed; I always knew I would die. It's just that the date had been moved up. That sort of reasoning doesn't work at all, by the way. As though death is something written on the calendar, to be crossed out and rescheduled like a dental cleaning.

After my bath, I lay naked on the bed. I think I may have tried to get an erection, I'm not sure. Though to comfort myself I almost certainly held it. I remember touching the hair, fingering the strands and imagining myself as a Neanderthal. Perhaps this experience would have been easier in those times, just to feel tired one day, then after a few, painful weeks in the most windless part of the cave, closer to the fire than ever before, with the choicest meat, to be immortalized in a ceremony of flame and shadow.

Anyway, that was part of the first day.

16.

In the afternoon, I left town for country.

My wife has always been overly perceptive. In order to hide the panic that was surely coming, I needed to get out of the apartment and scribbled a lie to say I was driving to our cottage in Amagansett after feeling inspired for a new story.

When Hadley texted me that night, I was seventy miles east of the city, at the old farm table in the kitchen with the lights off and my coat still on. The drive east had been uneventful. Just some minor flooding on Montauk Highway, as though my unshed tears were pooling elsewhere.

My wife texted to ask if I was coming back later in

the week so she could arrange dinner for us at Sant Ambroeus with friends we hadn't seen in a while.

I replied that I wasn't but hoped to see her at the weekend. This was true but also a lie.

On my second day at the cottage, I woke up with no sense of where I was or what had happened. Then I felt the thump of waves beyond the hedgerow and the previous day's news broke over me, drenching the bed, flooding the bedroom with a silent, churning panic.

The thought occurred to me that I should kill myself, erroneously thinking it might solve everything, when actually it would make things infinitely worse for *her*. In addition to grief would be guilt— which, like an anchor, she would drag through the rest of her life.

Not the legacy I wished to leave.

15.

YOU MIGHT BE wondering about relations, where they come into all this. We had friends of course (though Hadley and I were each other's best friends) but there was no extended family. My parents divorced when I was in my first year of university. My mother went back to Jamaica and died a decade later at her cousin's house in Montego Bay from a hemorrhagic stroke. The funeral was bright and somewhat happy—not what Hadley and I expected at all. After the divorce, my father went on to have another family—and, at the insistence of his new wife, gave up contact with anyone he knew (or loved) before they met. Last I heard he was accounting in Glasgow.

Hadley's mother succumbed to Alzheimer's in her late-sixties and died with no idea who she was or that she had a daughter. In the early years of the disease, she would even forget what had happened with her husband, and sit waiting for him to come home with a plate of dinner in the oven.

Anyway, we got through it all together as we had every tragedy since Hadley was thirteen, which was when we had our first serious conversation.

On my way to the chemistry block, school bag in hand, I heard something from the bicycle sheds and went to look. It was teenage Hadley. Completely alone. She saw it was me and didn't turn away. I approached and she held out a hand, which I took and cupped like an injured bird. The skin around her eyes was streaked with red from where she'd wiped the tears with her sleeve. You won't believe this, but teenage me put my arms around teenage Hadley. I remember the synthetic wool of her green school cardigan, the warmth and pliable softness of her body underneath. I knew what had happened, of course. Everyone in school was talking about how her father had crashed his car into the village sweet shop—though it was the heart attack before that killed him.

While Hadley was in my arms, I imagined him there, hovering over us, wearing the clothes he died in, a flickering form pushing, *pushing* into my heart all the things he would never say and do for his daughter.

After some moments, the biology teacher, Mr. Cummings, appeared and shouted at us to stop whatever "disgusting things" we were up to.

I waited for Hadley after school and walked with her back to the blue bungalow she had grown up in. Her mother was home but still asleep. Hadley made me a Marmite sandwich and a cup of tea. Then we went into her bedroom and sat with our backs against the wardrobe listening to Joy Division and New Order. We weren't really talking, but I felt she wanted me there. I remember my socks were gray and Hadley had on green school tights.

It's not that we fell in love—more like we had always loved each other and were then just remembering.

14.

WHAT I NEEDED in those early days was time alone to get past the swirling waste of my emotions, play over the many scenarios in my mind for what happens next, then decide the best course of action.

Mercifully, Hadley was unable to drive out to the cottage that first weekend. A friend was in town from Atlanta, and they were trying to organize brunch at a trendy bistro.

I can't remember everything I did then, but didn't go out much.

I do vaguely recall hours spent staring at objects I had never really looked at before, such as my wife's running shoes and the short socks stuffed into them.

I realized that for most of my life I had been dis-tracted by the administration of my desires, which I had never truly allowed myself to evaluate. It was as though I had been a bystander, a voyeur who contrib-utes ideas but who has no real hand in governance. That person was gone now.

Ironic how the fleeting nature of time compels us to act, yet is indifferent to our chronic inaction.

I was eating small meals, sandwiches, bowls of cereal, soup, fruit, and drinking herbal infusions—anything to comfort my nerves. I also understood how at heart I was a coward, unable to accept my coming death without panic, nausea, and wild fits of crying.

I believe it was the third day I took a long walk on the beach. After a mile or so it began to rain. At first I was annoyed, but then stood at the water's edge and stared at all the thousands of drops melting into the sea.

It happened quickly, the realization.

I'll do my best to convey what I felt, though I proceed with some reluctance, for you may see my epiphany as the desperation of a condemned man. And while the notion is less clear to me than it was that day on the beach, it still offers comfort. Of course the idea remains plausible, but it's as though the body wishes me to forget, the way it sweeps away dreams, leaving only crumbs.

What I experienced was the awareness of a deeper presence, like a soul—but different in that it was not another self, but something beyond identity and outside of feeling, like an un-self that was not limited by physical or temporal boundaries, a fragment of some larger whole that was neither living nor dead. It simply *was* the way the universe *is*.

To put it another way, I understood with certainty that everything *I* was going through was actually happening to Max. And up until that moment on the sand I had identified solely as Max, believing everything he felt to be things I was feeling; everything he was afraid of, things that were actually frightening and not merely elements of our world beyond Max's control.

Standing there, a lone figure in the rain, I was released from a kind of spiritual paralysis, and as a result, felt compassion for what Max was going through. He would need my help to get through this experience he had been told was "death." I must forgive him for being afraid and help him understand that Max was really little more than one of Plato's shadows, mistaken by all for the thing itself.

I knew that to permanently negate the incumbent, Max, was not sustainable. How could I convince Hadley that she was not really who she thought she was? That none of us are, and it's this fierce attachment to a made-up self that causes us to suffer?

Alas, over the next day or so I became Max again, albeit with the knowledge that in times of anguish I could spiritually detach and (referring to myself in the third person) observe with benign indifference the pain endured by all living things to enable permanence.

13.

WHEN YOU NURTURE the ability to witness your life in the third person, in extremis, or through prayer or meditation, there is an unavoidable shift in consciousness as you realize that who you are is not simply how you feel—but a presence beyond desire of any sort. Intense emotions that have held us prisoner all our lives suddenly lose power, are uncloaked as tricks of memory, exposed as tireless, groping sensations whose function is to keep us distracted by the body's appetites until the body is no more.

As you might have done, too, I returned to the beach each day after, hoping to experience the certainty I had felt that moment in the pouring rain.

By then, the news was settling and with it came the stark realization that Hadley would simply not survive my (Max's) absence from the life we (they) had built together.

I knew this for sure, because all the strength a person unknowingly sets aside for that sort of loss had been used up by the loss of our son, Adam.

I'm going to end this chapter early because I want to think about him for a while. It hurts, of course, but it's the most wonderful pain because it means he did not spend a single day of his short life unloved.

12.

THERE WAS SOMETHING in his body that couldn't be fixed. He had no idea of course—Adam was just an infant.

I use the word *just* foolishly, I know, believing I can anesthetize the sentence. And notice how I employ the term *infant*, from the Latin *infantem* (meaning speechless), as opposed to *baby*, from late Middle English (to mimic a child's first attempts at speech).

So often as an author I've witnessed the evasive power of language. How meaning does not come from single words, but from words in the context of other words, which would be impossible without single words to make up the sentence.

*****

When the doctors were certain, we were given the chance to take Adam home until the end. My wife didn't ask my opinion and I just agreed because I was too afraid of making the wrong decision—even though there is no such thing, apparently, in these situations.

In the months after Adam's cremation, Hadley and I almost split.

Our near separation was not because we didn't love each other, but because it hurt to love anything.

Eventually, we found a way to live but it took a lot of counseling, exhaustive cycles of talking, and many days of the dense fog that numbs you to everything but keeps hopelessness at bay (nights being the worst, as you may well know).

In the end, we found a way to harness grief to logic: *Would baby Adam have wanted his mother and father to suffer because of him?* And so, to honor his spirit, we stayed together, and in time realized it was what we wanted, too. That's not to say the sadness doesn't sometimes break free; it still happens and those days are hard, no matter how much time passes.

But now you can understand how it was another thing that helped me to cope. Adam was out there somewhere, and soon enough, I would be out there, too.

11.

I am transfixed by this perfect square of deep blue. It's possible that no solid object exists between the glass and infinity—that is to say the very edge of the observable universe, which would take 46 billion years to reach, traveling at the speed of light, which is 186,000 miles per second. And that's just what we can *see*. To get fractionally closer I'm raising my bed. I've been in one position for so long, I think my foot may have gone on ahead, as I can no longer feel it.

I wonder as I write this sentence if you are alive. And if those we lose come back to the place you're reading this from. Maybe they are near us all the time and we don't even know. There's more evidence for reincarnation than for the existence of god.

Consider for a moment that those we've lost do return. I read somewhere that grief is the distillation of memory and desire. But neither memory, nor desire, acknowledged our son Adam before he was conceived. So why do I trust these faculties now? It's unsettling to think that loving someone depends on our ability to remember them. If the feeling we call love wasn't reliant on memory, then men who have children they don't know about would *feel* their existence in the world.

And so without memory, the conventional definition of love is not possible. Therefore, what we call love is merely a survival mechanism bordering on narcissism—despite the power we ascribe to it.

Let's play a game.

Imagine that part of my illness means losing my ability to remember *now,* while I'm alive.

Would I forget my wife? Yes. Adam, too? Certainly—I would lose what little I have of him, even though the event of his life would still have taken place.

And herein lies another reason not to fear dying.

Bear with me now, because it's more than just a concept or some conceited form of escapism. For even though memory dies, the events—though not remembered—still took place.

Perhaps, then, it is only nature that has a memory of memory.

But what form could a record of what's forgotten take?

Look around. Better yet, push your hands through the skin of a river; lay down in any field; spread amidst the roots of trees; inhale dusk.

If those we've lost return here, we can't rely on memory to help us recognize them, which means there's only one thing to do: if you want to keep loving the ones you claim to have lost, you must be willing to love everyone.

Because anybody could be anybody. Even you are not who you *think* you are, at least in part. Which means even the most seemingly abhorrent creature is worthy of love.

Or no one is, ever.

And so, if you truly wish to *love* beyond the tricks of memory, there can be no distinction between the cockroach and the kitten, a stranger's child and your very own progeny.

That's how it has to work. Otherwise, it's a con. And what you claim is love, is nothing more than the survival mechanism I mentioned: a reaction to fear, a permissible narcissism, a prelude to self-pity.

So release any love you've been withholding.

Set it loose upon all living things. Then wait.

Those you grieve will find their way back to you in a form that makes it possible.

Woof.

Meow.

Scuttle.

Buzz.

Squeak.

Got any spare change?

Of course, they won't know at first who, or what, you are, only that the world is suddenly more beautiful.

If you think this is all unbelievable and you'll be spared the suffering of myself and Hadley, this gradual breaking down of everything you love (in the conventional sense) until there's nothing left—not even someone to remember when there *was* something—then I suggest you put this story away until the time of that first panic, when your eyes are finally open and your life is suddenly coming apart like a tissue in water.

I'll be waiting.

Right here on this page where you left me. A dropped seed.

And then I promise we will grow, and you will prosper as fiercely as you wither.

10.

I MANAGED TO get through that first weekend alone at the cottage without saying anything out of the ordinary. Hadley later ascribed my altered state to an excess of time spent at my computer, working out the details of a new story, which I suppose is true.

When you are in possession of knowledge that would shatter the person you adore if they knew, you love them more by realizing that every small thing they do—from eating ice cream to laughing at something on television to asking your opinion about a hairstyle—is no longer a small thing but some grand event in the universe. It's like you've already died, but somehow been able to come back and appreciate what's truly precious.

I warn you, though, there is loneliness in knowing.

9.

My ROOM GLOWS with the majesty of Wednesday.

On a little table where Hadley sets her magazines and Jeremy puts the case for his glasses when he reads, is the small stack of books I have written. I peer at them with slight embarrassment, but also gratitude, because writing them gave more than it took. And part of me is inside each story with a part of you, the reader. It's like the memory you might have of the house you grew up in, except what you don't realize is that I grew up there, too, along with many others.

I think if you could feel my hospital room as I feel it, in the arms of this moment—you'd be quite comfortable and not afraid.

Outside, dawn has washed the sky, which means I'm probably going to live another day, giving us time to get back to the story of how I eventually told Hadley. Remember, we do not wake from dreams into reality, but into other dreams.

8.

THREE WEEKS AFTER the diagnosis, Hadley still didn't know. When I returned to see my doctor for different medication, she suggested I find an end-of-life therapist. This seemed exciting because it meant I wasn't the only one. There was an entire industry based on terminal illness.

Fantastic!

During our third session, Carol asked me about suicide.

Of course, you remember I had discounted this as an option long before, for the simple reason that it's not the dead who suffer, but the living.

"I was in bed. In the country. The window was open. I could hear the sea."

"How did that make you feel, Max? Hearing the sea?"

"Scared."

"Would you be open to exploring why?"

"Because things we had experienced together would always remind her of my absence."

"That's right. After your passing, she will have to reinterpret everything—learn to see it again without you."

"Will that help?"

"Only if she allows the old associations to recede. She has to *want* to give you up."

I remember looking at my shoes then. I would never buy another pair. The shoes and clothes and glasses and hats I owned were the only ones I would ever have.

"So, ten years from now, my wife could be a completely different person? One who might not even love me anymore?"

Carol acknowledged my pain with her eyes. "Isn't that why you're here?" She passed me a tissue box. "If Hadley is to survive your loss, Max, she'll have to start again, or go back to the time before she knew you—and take it from there."

"It seems unfair."

"That we suffer, Max?"

"No, that suffering is contagious."

"That takes us to a deeper truth few people will ever confront."

"Which is what?"

"That only the fortunate suffer. Most are damned to indifference or blinded by the fantasy of life after death."

"I think there is life after death."

"Would you be comfortable telling me about that, Max?"

"We don't remember, of course, but our life energy gets recycled."

"Like reincarnation?"

"Yes, but without karma. That just seems like another attempt to control the living."

"Interesting," Carol said, smiling, "but not very consoling if you don't remember."

"To be honest, I think it's better that we forget, otherwise we would be consumed by desires. The loss of Max at death is akin to an act of love. Because it's memory that makes the living suffer."

"Are you religious, Max?"

"Oh no, I'm just a lapsed atheist. But it was that experience on the beach I told you about that got me into all this."

"Have you had a chance to explore Buddhism?"

"Buddhism is especially interesting to me, once you can get past the robes and ten syllable words. But it's the overlapping concepts in all religions that I find reassuring, but also fairly frustrating."

"How is that?"

"Well, for instance, I've been reading a translation of the Qur'an, which says, 'Do not be deceived by the life of this world.' A sentiment I can safely say is echoed through every religion I've encountered. Now, with so much overlap it amazes me the lengths people go to imposing separation and creating disorder just so they can leverage power over others. It makes me angry."

"I can understand why it would, but try and see the bigger picture, Max."

"You mean historically?"

"Not quite. Listen to this story. When I was in the last year of my undergraduate degree, I hired some decorators to paint my new apartment. They were Navajo. When the work was finished, they had done a beautiful job, but in each room had left a tiny square at the top of the wall unpainted. When I asked about this, they said the gods enter our lives through imperfection, and so it would be better for me to leave it."

"Did you?"

Carol laughed, "Yes, reluctantly, but today I'm grateful for what they did." Then she paused. "In the same way, you must learn to reconcile your ideal world with the one we live in."

"I'm trying, but I get upset when I think about how Hadley will suffer."

"My father used to say to watch those we love suffer without being able to do anything is to know how god feels."

"Was he religious?"

"Only when things were outside of his control. Anyway, it's good you've made all this progress on your own."

"You should have seen me a few weeks ago."

"Well, Max, that's arguably the most challenging time. When a person feels most alone, singled out, even."

"But I still haven't told Hadley. I want to have a plan before I do . . . because of our experience with Adam."

"Your son?"

"Yes. I can't change what's happening to me, or what happened to him, but I can affect how my death changes her life once I'm gone. Do you think that's possible?"

"It can be our goal, Max. I have some suggestions for you to weigh up, but is there anything you had in mind? You know her better than anyone."

Carol was wonderful. For the next few months, I saw her twice per week. She had a deep voice, a smoker's voice, and cropped black hair. She had grown up in Harlem, and her office on Central Park West was a place of cushions, wicker, and 1970s paperbacks.

With unintended professionalism, Carol died of a heart attack the same week I entered the hospital and would therefore no longer have been able to visit her office. There was a small obituary in the newspaper. She had trained with a prominent Ashkenazi psychotherapist in Berlin, studied in India for three years in the 1970s with a guru, written five books published by the University of Michigan Press, had no living family, and had willed everything to a small, privately funded group home in Kentucky that offered shelter to battered women.

And so now, over the top of this book, in the world of moving figures where my wife currently dwells, any happiness Hadley feels, despite everything she's gone through, is partly because of Carol. It's important to say that, to acknowledge the people who've helped us. I hope to meet Carol again in another form. Or perhaps that's what it was, a reunion of sorts. And with this story, I'm giving (back) to you what was given to me, and we keep going around like this, doomed to have forgotten why we forget.

7.

To SAY I accepted my death would be inaccurate.

Instead, I began to acknowledge a coming change, which hinged on admitting I have no idea what death is . . . beyond memory lost. I started to imagine my life as water cupped, momentarily, from an endless sea that isn't in the universe but is the universe itself.

And so, after a few weeks of planning during my sessions with Carol, it was decided how I would tell my wife.

Dinner first.

I would make sure Hadley ordered something unusual, as she would most likely never eat it again. But I wanted there to be a meal, a last supper of ignorance. Happiness would come later, when she herself woke up and realized how blessed we had been to have embraced each other freely. If you haven't realized: happiness as we know it is only possible as the anticipation of itself, or as a memory, which renders it completely imaginary. (Note how I use the penultimate word in that sentence for emphasis, which ironically implies doubt.)

And so I've come to rely on faith. But you have to have faith there's faith to have faith.

So then, it was a matter of faith—as in hope and certainty—that we would meet again somewhere in the universe, if I were able to convince her—after my death—to love without reservation.

Perhaps that's why I'm writing this.

I was not going to tell Hadley in the restaurant if that's what you're thinking. Just play out the scene as if it were you and your partner, and you'll soon realize how cruel a place it would be to announce demise, surrounded by other couples in the midst of their tacit avoidance.

It had to be at home, where she could safely fall to pieces.

But I didn't yet know where. Perhaps the kitchen? The laundry room? Someplace where she would not always think, *This is where Max told me*. There is nowhere that memory can't find, can't trickle in. That's why in my will I have set aside money and suggested Hadley use it to have our beach house remodeled. That was something I'd talked about in therapy with Carol. I wanted to give Hadley a chance to restructure what had been ours into something imperatively hers.

After my diagnosis, I began visiting our seaside cottage more often, ostensibly to work on my new big project. And on weekends, my wife would drive out in her white sports car. You know you love someone when, at the sound of tires rolling over small stones in the driveway, you inflate like a balloon.

The day I was to make my announcement, Hadley arrived from the city as usual. It was Friday evening. I went outside to carry in the duffel bag she would always stuff with clothes and magazines. It was brown and had an exterior pocket for her tennis racquet.

"How was the traffic?" I asked, opening the hood of the car for her bag. But she was already halfway up the steps.

"Fine," she replied over her shoulder, "once I got through Queens."

When she was in the house, I climbed into the driver's seat. Touched the thick wheel, still warm where her hands had been moments before. I closed both eyes and inhaled the scent of lavender hand cream.

By the early hours of tomorrow morning our old lives would be over. We would be different people in a different house—dead without having died.

Inside, I dropped Hadley's bag by the umbrella stand and called her name. No reply. Then I heard the upstairs bathroom flush. I took the steps slowly and drifted into the bedroom. She was removing her shoes by reaching around and pulling from the heel.

"Want to lay down for a minute?" she asked, falling back onto the feather duvet.

It was something I wanted, but was afraid to bring up, in light of my plans.

We didn't need to draw the shades as in the city because our house was quite far from any others, with an expanse of olive-green marshland where the pool house ended. Over the years, we had made love many times in that pool house. We'd sleep there, too, during the change in season when it was too cool for mosquitoes but remnants of summer lingered, like those birds that sing after dark.

In November, with the pool closed, we lay out blankets and read novels in heavy sweaters. Winter was coming. We could taste it in our mouths. Occasionally there would be gunshots. Hunters in the marshes on flat boats. It was the only time Hadley used the f-word. To describe those men.

I didn't realize it at that time, but I think the ducks were somehow connected to what had happened with our son. Hadley was not vegetarian and so her malice always seemed without logic.

For a while we just lay there on the feather duvet, bodies touching. Seagulls flashing at the window. I wonder if, in her mind, Hadley was going over her own flight from the city that evening.

Then we got under the covers.

Hadley took off her clothes and dropped each item by the side of the bed. I did the same. I remember seeing her glossy bra and panties on the floor and feeling sad again. I didn't know what sex would be like once she knew, and so I tried to rejoin the moment.

There would soon come a time—as early as twelve months—when I wouldn't be able to do anything like this. I imagined we would just cuddle then. She would probably cry, and then later, alone in our apartment, she might lay on the bed, and through the thin fabric of her underwear, pleasure herself with the memory of pleasure.

When dusk filled the corners of our home, Hadley went downstairs to eat something, even though we would be sitting in the restaurant within an hour. It was a peculiar habit of hers that used to irritate me. But lying there with the warm imprint of her body in the sheets, I laughed at how ridiculous everything was, and how annoying habits are as precious as anything else, if not more.

Half an hour later I was shaving when Hadley appeared in the doorway wearing a green dress, black stockings, and patent-leather shoes.

"What do you think, Max?"

"Very nice indeed."

"Oh, you always say that. It doesn't mean anything."

"Okay then," I said, taking in as much as I could. "You look like Maid Marian as a hooker who won the lottery."

She laughed, and I was glad because it would have been so easy for her to say something cruel that later, when I was gone, would become a source of torment.

It was dark when we left the house to go have dinner. A southeasterly wind was howling off the sea. We could taste the salt. I opened the passenger door for my wife and watched her get in. The way she adjusted her tights was a stark reminder of not only what I was losing, but how much I had been given—and that I should be more grateful than bitter, not only for what had happened, but for all the things that hadn't happened.

On the drive to Nick & Toni's Restaurant, Hadley gave her usual instructions on how *not* to use the gear paddles behind the steering wheel. My eyes sparkled with glee. I was even delighted to circle the parking lot for five minutes so that we could get the closest possible parking space to the door of the restaurant. Hopefully, she would also ask several times if I had locked the car, when she had seen the lights flash and heard the double chirp.

These rituals of marriage that you learn to accept if you wish the relationship to thrive, I've since realized in extremis, are indicators of an uncommon intimacy. Their purpose? The transfiguration of unarticulated fear into shared moments of trust.

When we got to the restaurant, the maître d' was new and didn't know us by sight. We were shown to our table as though we'd never been there before, as though it were our first time. The erasure had already begun.

There was a small vase with sprigs of purple heather in the center of our table. The linens were starched and pressed. A woman in black clogs and a charcoal apron appeared holding menus. When she announced the special entrée that evening as local duck, I felt a kick under the table.

"I was actually thinking lobster," my wife said, "with a glass of champagne."

We didn't always have money. When we left England, it was with Oxfam suitcases and just enough in traveler's checks to rent an apartment for three months on Ludlow Street. Hadley was still writing her thesis and I worked in a bar pretending to be Jack Kerouac. I would bring home leftover Salisbury steak and tater tots in a Styrofoam container. I saved my tips to pay for her tennis club, as there were some luxuries I wouldn't let go.

Around this time, I sold my first short story to the *Bulgarian Review*.

Without consulting Hadley, I cashed the small check and went to a racetrack just north of the city. Foolish, I know, but I was young and empowered by the fact that I would soon be a published author. Other publications would follow, big national magazines scoured by literary agents for fresh blood. But there's something hallowed about a writer's first acceptance letter—even when it comes from Bulgaria, which most people don't know is the original home of the Thracians.

The only experience I had with gambling was from reading Charles Bukowski. For better or worse, I bet my entire earnings on *A Very Freaky Chicken* in race four.

It was pouring rain, and I couldn't believe the horses were still going to run, but they did, and against massive odds, my faith in *A Very Freaky Chicken* was rewarded, because the favorites had pulled out before the race due to conditions underfoot. My bet paid out almost eighteenfold. I stuffed the cash in my pocket and ran out before I could do something impulsive.

Since we had been teenagers, bopping in our rooms to The Smiths, I had promised Hadley a trip to Paris and so I booked it the moment I returned home. Although we would have very little spending money over the three-day French vacation, I wanted us to have something we would never forget.

Of course, I realize now that everything is destined to be forgotten. But believing that it *wouldn't* gave it a significance it could only truly achieve years later with the certainty that it *would.*

I found an inexpensive bed and breakfast aptly named Le Coq near Gare du Nord station. The room was so small that if one person was standing, the other had to sit on the bed. And the mattress was very soft, which made getting up a comedy. There were mirrors on the closet doors, which we made use of, despite always being tired from walking. That tiny, worn out hotel was one of the places I've felt happiest in my life. I remember it clearly, from the electric hairdryer on the wall to a green vase of plastic flowers on the desk. You have to realize: I had just sold my first story. In a few months, hundreds, if not thousands of Bulgarians would be reading my words, following characters I had brought into the world from nothing. The truth was that a team of esteemed Balkan men and women of letters had found my thoughts original enough to share.

Even if no one liked it, the narrative would live forever on dusty library shelves, waiting to be discovered by people with taste. My story could never be unpublished. There was nothing to be afraid of anymore, no insult capable of denting my happiness. My short story had been accepted for publication. And unless the world ended before November, I could never *not* be a writer.

That's how young I was.

In truth, it's probably safe to say that the greatest writers among us never get published. The ones we know are but a splinter on the tree of the ones we didn't recognize, or put in prison, or murdered, or feebly rejected with the same scribbled note—*Sorry. Not right for us*—because their work did not conform to the current fashion.

On our second day in Paris, we walked along a street of fashion boutiques. Hadley fell in love with a pair of suede ballet flats with heart cutouts that she saw in a store window. We were like Audrey Hepburn and Gregory Peck in *Roman Holiday*, except we were in Paris staying at Le Coq. When it rained, we went into a bakery for coffee and she talked about the shoes. I listened. "I have never seen shoes like that before," she said. "And suede is quite durable. Very easy to clean."

When the rain stopped, we went to a park where other couples were strolling up and down the gravel paths. The air was fresh after all that water. With the same confidence that led me to believe in *A Very Freaky Chicken*, I stood and told Hadley I had left something in the bakery. "Wait for me beside that carousel," I said, pointing. "Choose a horse for when I get back."

If I ran, I knew it would only take five minutes to reach the river, and the shoe shop wasn't far beyond that on Rue du Faubourg Saint-Honoré.

On our last evening, we discovered a flight of old stone steps that led down to the Seine. We found a place to sit on a low wall, then took turns ripping flames of croissant from a paper bag. There were metal hoops in the wall once used for tying boats. We could feel the coolness of stone on our legs. Hardly able to wait any longer, I rummaged in my shoulder bag for the bundle wrapped in rose-colored tissue.

"What's that?" she asked. I think she knew but wanted to make sure it wasn't something useless like soap.

When I gave it to her, she just looked at me with the package in her hands.

"I thought we agreed no gifts, Max?"

"It's just something small."

What Hadley didn't know was that our trip to Paris had really been paid for by *A Very Freaky Chicken*, not the literati of Bulgaria.

"But I didn't get you anything except that stupid watering can."

"There's no need. My literary career has been endorsed by the sixteenth largest country in Europe."

She softened at my look of satisfaction and carefully unwrapped the bundle to reveal suede shoes with heart cutouts.

"Put them on," I said. And she did, wrapping her old shoes carefully in the tissue because they were special, too, in how they had brought us to this moment.

Nearby, under the bridge, some homeless men were sitting on blankets. A glass bottle was being picked up and put down. Instead of being afraid, I felt these men were a natural part of us and delighted in their steady voices and laughter like low bubbling. The river, too, was soft and magnificent.

We walked back to the hotel with our hands locked. I don't think we spoke then. I can't recall any words— just the sound of our shoes on the street, moving slowly in the direction of a bed where parts of us would die so that other parts could be born.

6.

WE THOUGHT WE were old then, but that's because we were young. One day, long after I'm gone, Hadley will convince herself that she is young. This will happen when she's old, and the actual hours we spent together in Paris are but a tiny fraction of the time she has spent there since, in memory.

5.

WHAT AN EVENING it was turning out to be. Making love at dusk with seagulls circling. The wind outside moving leaves and lifting our hair, as though searching for something. Then in the restaurant, the lobster—oh, what things it must have seen in the depths before coming red and hot to our table like an angry thumb. Then, listening to my wife; her seriousness about things she would soon realize were unserious.

When the waiter came to remove our dishes, I noticed someone across the small dining room watching us. He was about my age, and sitting with a blond in a lilac wrap dress and boots that reminded me of Peter Pan.

I insisted on dessert and ordered the only two things I knew my wife would like. Immediately I realized my mistake: I should have asked for cookies and the crème caramel, both of which she would never want again. But it would have looked odd to change the order, so I let it go.

My wife's hands were resting on the table then. I reached over and enclosed them. I had known those hands for so long. Watched them wrinkle over time like sheets of delicate paper, written on by life. Within one hour she would receive the worst news imaginable. The final knot in a string of disasters that held together each decade of her life. Then I realized someone was standing over us. It was the man who had been staring.

"Sorry to interrupt . . ." he said, glancing blankly at me before turning his attention fully to Hadley. "But I simply had to come over."

His dining companion, the blond woman, was also turned toward us, grinning with perfect Hollywood teeth.

"Oh my god," said my wife, pushing back her chair to stand. "Alan?"

"I know," said the man. "What are the chances? After all these years." They embraced.

Hadley seemed genuinely surprised. "I can't believe you recognized me."

Instinctively I rose and the man shook my hand vigorously, as though congratulating me for winning a prize.

"Max, this is Alan, my neighbor from growing up. Can you believe it?"

His mouth was now open with surprise and delight. Then he motioned for the woman to join us.

"Hi!" she said, striding over in her tall boots. "I'm Daphne."

The man had thinning hair, but the excitement in his voice was vibrant and boyish. Perhaps he had only recognized Hadley after acknowledging the attractiveness of a stranger. I think Daphne could see that, too, which was why she introduced herself with just a name. I learned later she was the man's ex-wife, and they had dinner every Friday when he drove out from Dumbo to pick up their teenage sons for the weekend.

As you know, I became acquainted with my wife at a very young age, and while it took me years to actually speak to her, I felt I was intimate with all the details of her life, even the minutiae. Alan must have lived next door before she and I were close, that is—before her father's death. She had never mentioned him. Or maybe I had forgotten. *She* certainly had, forgotten I mean, as I could tell it was a surprise for Hadley to find him dining in the same restaurant, still neighbors in a way.

When the maître d' and a waiter brought over two chairs, Daphne and Alan sat down. A moment later the waitress appeared with our desserts and four spoons. I watched her put them down on the table as though she was dealing a hand of cards.

Only moments before I had cupped my wife's hands, readying them to hatch in this new world.

4.

HOLD ON, THE corridor outside my hospital room is suddenly busy with footsteps and tall carts. Either someone has died or it's breakfast. Not sure which is worse, to be honest.

The doctor will come soon to glance over my charts and chat with me. She knows I'm mostly alone. And that it is only a matter of weeks—maybe days.

Maybe today.

Maybe in five minutes.

If it is today, at least we're together now.

You and me.

You might have guessed what I'm implying with all this—or perhaps you're in the dark.

Threaded into the story of me telling my wife the news of my illness is a separate narrative, that you may not be enjoying because you find it far-fetched, which would be ironic if I am correct and you are are (partly or entirely) composed of the same energy typing these words here *now* in this hospital, years before you were (quite possibly) born.

Or perhaps you are animated by the same energy (partly or entirely) that composed my wife? Or (partly or entirely) our son, Adam, or the bully that brought us together—though Adam, or Hadley, or Max, or the bully is not your name now.

You may not have a name.

Is it so ridiculous to think that you could be reading something *at this moment* that you wrote long ago?

Partly or entirely?

Consider that language is always one step ahead: read words attain meaning through the life experience of the reader, not the author. Remember how a person's life is like water cupped momentarily from the bottomless bowl of the universe? And how when the vessel tires, the water returns, only to be scooped again, partly or entirely?

You can't say I haven't at least laid the groundwork.

I know you probably wouldn't say it to my face,

but even if you do believe all this is simply the washed-out philosophy of a dying man trying to bargain his way back into life—even one without memory—because the idea of living again mitigates fear of impending nothingness, then just let me go on. Give me that luxury. Please. There isn't much I've asked for these past few months (except for small things like Marmite).

Truthfully, I didn't believe in any of this two years ago. Though, to be honest, that was probably because I had never thought about it.

I knew this day would come—I just thought Hadley and I would be old, bedridden eccentrics who chew with their mouths open and keep the radio turned up to eleven.

Sometimes I wonder if we're not just tools for nature with the illusion of free will. Take that night when Alan and Daphne joined us for the last supper, for instance, the evening of my big reveal to Hadley. Maybe it wasn't a chance encounter, but nature insisting on Hadley's survival in the form of a horny dentist and a magnanimous ex-wife.

Oh, bugger, hold on . . . someone is looking at me through the mesh window in the door.

It's the doctor.
Knocks while entering, as usual.
All smiles, as usual.

Time passes.

The doctor came in to say she'd be back at the end of her rounds. I hope she doesn't return when Hadley and Jeremy are here. I like to enjoy their company in peace, not while being probed like an undercooked chicken.

Twenty minutes have elapsed since I typed that last sentence.

I've had some time to think.

I also fluffed my pillow and looked at my face in a small mirror beside my bed.

It's certainly not the face I remember as mine, I've lost so much weight. Physically, I shall die as a stranger to myself.

3.

"Tell me more," said Carol. "If you feel like it."

"Did I mention he was a dentist?"

"No, you didn't."

"Well, anyway, Alan and his ex-wife basically ruined everything."

"How so?"

"After such an unexpected surprise, I couldn't tell Hadley about my condition."

"Why is that, Max?"

"Well, in fiction it's usually understood that you can't have two big reveals in the same chapter . . . I think that's also true for life."

I paused as Carol jotted something down.

"Plus, they ended up coming back to our cottage, which was irritating . . . I mean, who drinks coffee at midnight?"

Carol sighed. "Oral surgeons, apparently. Do you have another plan for when you will tell her?"

"This weekend . . . but not if she gets her period."

Carol frowned. "And why is that?"

"Well, I want to avoid her associating it with bad news."

Carol nodded. "Wow. You've really thought this through."

I remember it made me feel good she said that. I *had* thought it through. I was going to die and I was controlling elements of the aftermath with thoughtfulness and dignity.

"Though sometimes," I remember admitting. "I do feel I'm a coward, which is perhaps why I'm putting it off."

"If you were a coward, Max, I don't think you'd be here now. Cowardice, or the fear of it, might be something we can trace to an event in childhood, a sense of powerlessness carried over."

"Oh, I'm sure," I said. "But there's little point in going into all that now."

I didn't have to explain why. Carol was great like that. She laughed, then reached for her box of menthol cigarettes, which meant our time was up.

As I was saying goodbye, Carol knocked her coffee, spilling it over the glass-topped table.

"Oh flup," she said. "Would you mind telling my next appointment I'll be a few moments?"

In the waiting room I found a man slightly younger than myself. Clean shaven but with hair in a messy side part.

"Carol asked if you'd wait a few minutes."

"Is everything okay?"

"She spilled some coffee and is cleaning it up."

"Oh. Thanks for letting me know," he said, sweeping his hair to one side. "I don't know what I'd do without Carol."

"Me neither."

The man stood and extended his hand. "I'm Jeremy Abrams."

"How do you do?" I replied, shaking his hand. "Max Little."

"The writer?"

You can imagine how thrilled I was.

But then Carol ruined the moment by suddenly appearing with a roll of paper towels. She looked at us without saying a word, then disappeared back into her office. The man turned and followed her in.

"Wish me luck, Max."

As I waited for the elevator it suddenly occurred to me that Jeremy Abrams might also be dying (despite his abundance of hair).

Downstairs, I told the doorman I was waiting for my wife. He nodded, but it was obvious he didn't care or suspect I was planning to ambush one of Carol's other patients.

I sat on a bench in the faux-medieval lobby and wondered if Jeremy Abrams would find it unsettling that I waited for him. I was taking a risk. I knew that. He might even tell Carol and she'd stop seeing me.

But if this Abrams fellow was dying, too, I wanted to talk and listen and try to understand what it was like for him. Perhaps he had told his wife or partner and would be willing to share some crucial advice that might help me and, more importantly, help Hadley.

Anyway, this is how Jeremy came into our lives.

2.

JEREMY SPOTTED ME immediately as he exited the elevator, but did not seem nervous or put out.

"Did you forget something, Max?"

"No," I said, looking to see if the doorman was out of earshot. "I actually wanted a word with you."

"About Carol?"

"I wanted to say that if you ever feel like talking, then—"

"Yes," he said, cutting me off. "Do you have time now?"

I nodded. "We could walk in the park."

When we got outside the wind stung our cheeks and burrowed into our clothes. We pulled up the collars on our jackets, then waited for a break in the traffic.

"Thank you for suggesting this," Jeremy said as we crossed the four lanes of Central Park West. "There's no one in my life who can relate to what I'm going through. Literally everyone in my family has their head in the sand."

It turned out that Jeremy was not dying. His mother was.

He had never known his father and the extended family, younger sisters, nieces and nephews, all out in New Jersey, were not taking the news well. Jeremy had started seeing Carol to get ideas that would help them and his mother feel less afraid.

"What about you?" I asked. "How are you coping?"

He smiled as a squirrel darted out in front of us. "I was fine until I started seeing Carol."

"Oh really?" I said, surprised that sessions with Carol could make someone feel worse.

"No, I mean the truth is that I was probably messed up and just hiding it really well—from myself I mean. Now it's all on the table, Max. I've even started talking about my absent father."

After an hour of walking, I started to get tired. We were at the southern edge of the park, near the Plaza

Hotel where there are benches and vendors selling food in paper napkins to tourists.

"This morning you were a complete stranger," Jeremy said. "And now you know more about me than pretty much anyone."

"You're not married?"

"I was engaged, five years ago, to someone who worked at the United Nations. But she went back to Brussels and I couldn't leave my mother, so I guess it wasn't meant to be."

"Your mother is lucky to have you."

"Normally I would have talked to her about all this. I hope I haven't burdened you with my problems."

"Not at all," I said. "It's a relief not to feel so alone. Especially since the worst is still to come."

Jeremy put a hand on my shoulder.

"No, not dying," I laughed, "telling Hadley."

"Well, there's no getting around that one, Max. It's going to be bad."

"But at least I'll have a chance to reassure her and say everything I need to . . . her as well . . . even if it's painful."

Jeremy listened. It was still very cold, but I could tell he was taking it all in.

"Carol told me today, Max, that one way to manage my tough feelings is to practice daily forgiveness."

"But it's not your mother's fault, is it?"

"No, not my mother. I have to forgive myself for being messed up, forgive myself for feeling upset and unable to cope—for not wanting to go through it."

"Damn, that's good. I wonder why she hasn't suggested it for me yet." I joked, and thought Jeremy was laughing but when I turned saw that he was weeping. It was probably something he'd wanted to do for a long time in the company of another person.

We met several times over the next two weeks, taking turns to bring lunch, usually a sandwich or a bagel or chicken soup. Jeremy helped me prepare to tell Hadley, even offering to come over and sit in the building lobby when I finally broke the news. That's how close we were getting. It was actually Jeremy who suggested I start keeping this journal— he said it would be good for me to be in the habit of writing again.

When I told Hadley, it went as you might imagine.

I did it in the city, where there would be distractions for when the time came for us to go outside again.

I'm surprised the neighbors didn't call someone, some of the noises Hadley made. At first, she buried her face in a couch cushion and tore at the fabric with her nails. I sat motionless, watching her contort and writhe as though the illness had left my brain and was now taking control of her body.

Eventually, she got up and went slowly into the bedroom. I followed. It felt as though I had done something wrong. She got under the covers fully clothed. I couldn't see what she was doing, but I sat on the end of the bed and listened to the long, guttural moans— which reminded me of Grendel for some reason.

I think for a while Hadley didn't know I was in the room, but then she lowered the comforter and said my name several times—heaved it from her chest as if pulling the word through wet stones.

Lying down, I could see that her face was swollen with patches of red, and that tears had dried in the lines around her eyes, leaving a gossamer film.

We stayed like that until the dark came and we could no longer see one another.

Later, at some uncharted point of night, I woke and saw her at the desk, typing on the computer.

"I'm taking the next two weeks off," she said. Her voice was quiet but determined.

When I sat up it was obvious she had been awake for some time, trawling the internet to learn as much as she could about my condition.

"I'm afraid there are no alternative therapies," I said.

"Not true," she replied quickly. "There's one in South America with native healers. I'm looking into flights now."

Carol had warned me this might happen.

In the morning, there were several hard sessions of crying again. At one point she got down in front of the toilet, but nothing came up except a clear, stringy paste. After that she gained some composure and said she was sorry for any time in our marriage when she'd spoken harshly or been cruel. I told her that none came to mind, but that any difficult moments had brought us closer. She said she wished we could go back to when we were young and live it all over again.

She couldn't believe I was so calm. "It's a miracle," she said.

That made me feel good, as you and I both know the hell I'd been through to arrive at this place.

I reassured her that most of the paperwork had been done, and there was a list of names and email addresses of people she would need to contact to let them know, when it happened. The email had been written, and would be sent to her by our lawyer, along with things to sign for the life insurance and social security. I would also leave the passwords to my email and social media accounts so she could close them down. I told her it was important she did all this.

And my ashes were to be sprinkled, when she was ready, in the sea off Amagansett. And if she could smuggle some back to England—along the grass bank where she had saved me from the bully.

Around lunchtime on the second day, Hadley and I sat together on the couch with hot drinks.

"I just can't believe it," she said. "You look fine. I can't believe you're sick."

"I think I knew for a while. I felt it."

"Why didn't you say something?"

"Because I wasn't sure."

"You must have been frightened."

"I was frightened when I knew for certain."

"Why didn't you tell me?"

"Because I had to come to terms with it myself."

"It must have been awful, that first day."

"I actually came home and watered the plants. Then I walked around the apartment and looked at everything as though for the first time."

"I just wish I'd been there for you, at the beginning," she said.

"But this is how I wanted it."

She took up my hand and squeezed. "How about some lunch?"

"That's a great idea, seems like you're feeling better."

"I'm afraid that's just the part of me that still doesn't believe it." She laughed and the sound filled my entire body. I felt then she was going to live for many years after my death, and I wondered if this moment would be one she returned to often in memory.

After eating something we tried to watch a film. When it was over, I thought about mentioning that weekend at our cottage, the dinner when her childhood neighbor and his ex-wife interrupted, but decided to leave the evening as it was, intact, sealed off from this new, abridged version of our marriage.

"There's some time yet before I go into the hospice. We might have a few good months if you want us to travel."

"Hospice?"

"It's like a hotel, but there's no set checkout time."

"Oh, Max," she said. "I know what hospice is."

"It's actually in a part of the hospital, I can just call it that if you'd prefer."

She nodded weakly. "I'm going to leave work so I can be with you every second."

"Actually, I think you should keep your job, and go every day as usual." It was something I had already thought about. "Because you'll need work after it's happened as a distraction."

Hadley stood and left the room without saying where she was going. After a minute though, I heard her in the bathroom, vomiting up the soup and sandwiches we had ordered for lunch.

In the early part of the afternoon, when I felt Hadley was able to focus on what I was saying, I told her about Carol and the progress I'd made during our sessions. I also confessed how much comfort I had found from a new friend, an anesthesiologist fellow I met outside Carol's office.

I explained how we'd been going for walks in the park. Though I tried not to let my enthusiasm for this new relationship overtake the moment, which belonged to Hadley.

After that, we lay on the bed again. Let ourselves be distracted by other things in our lives, even laughing once or twice.

Unexpectedly, we made love.

Then lay touching—so still as to feel the day

beginning to exhale. People in the buildings around us were putting on coats to catch trains from Grand Central, or have a drink somewhere familiar before heading home. But we were at home in bed because I had only a short time left to live.

It actually felt as though time had stopped and we were porcelain figures with painted eyes and painted mouths, unmoved by the daily sweep of light, held in place by the weight of intimacy, locked into an eternal moment that would only end when we ceased to perceive it.

"I want to meet your doctor friend," Hadley said, sitting up. "Jeremy is it?"

I nodded.

"I feel like he's helped you, Max. I can tell—no one knows you like I do."

"He's wonderful—"

"Though I'm a bit jealous you told him before me."

"Jealous?"

"Yes, Max, but also, I suppose, rather grateful."

Some time later, Hadley felt sick again—this time it was a headache. But after a long hot shower it went away, leaving only a deep tiredness in its place.

Then evening came. Unable to face the long corridor of night, we took one sleeping pill each, and sunk to the very bottom of sleep, as far as we could get from the surface of our lives.

1.

LUNCH WASN'T BAD today.

I can still eat some things. But mostly I'm fed through a needle in my arm.

It could be anytime now.

In the middle of a sentence even.

You might turn the page and find only yourself.

To be honest, I've often thought I simultaneously belonged somewhere else. It's one of those things a lot of people feel but never talk about.

The first time it happened, I was four. My parents had taken me to a medieval village where actors dress in period costumes and talk about their crafts to anyone who stops to listen. There were animals, too, along with plows and carts. But it was the smell of hay baking in the sun that made me certain I was remembering something I couldn't remember. The feelings were simply beyond anything I could express as a child. It was like the certainty of something without the memory itself—a sense of being haunted.

One day people may be able to explain certain experiences like ghosts or déjà vu. But for you and me it's like looking through a keyhole into the sun.

Hadley and Jeremy are coming later today for sure. My wife first, then Jeremy will come once his obligations at the hospital end.

You might wonder what dying people look forward to. Being visited, yes, but also being left alone— though that takes a lot of practice, managing thoughts. I also meditate and I pray.

Thinking over the treasure of my life is another pleasure, raking through my best memories and sometimes coming across things I had overlooked or thought unimportant at the time. There are people I think about, too, some I've realized I still love but will never see again. I do wonder if some part of them will sense the moment I'm lifted from the world.

I also look forward to reassuring people it's okay this is happening. Something beautiful even, which reminds me of a story I heard or read somewhere. I think the tale comes from India, but it might be China, or Vietnam.

An old man is lying in his bed about to die. All around stand the members of his family. Closest to the man is his wife, and a little farther back are his grown children holding the hands of their offspring, the dying man's grandchildren.

Although the old man can't speak, in his mind he's pleading with his god to give him *more* life. He doesn't want to go. He's afraid what will happen to the people he loves so dearly after he's gone. He has had a wonderful life and yearns for more.

As always, god listens.

But then a moment before the man dies, god offers to grant his wish. The man can continue to live and stay with his family, but on one condition: the man must switch souls with the youngest of his grandchildren. If he agrees, the man will have exactly what he has pleaded for: the chance to live again with the people he loves most deeply.

It takes the old man no time at all to make a decision. Then he laughs along with god and dies with a satisfaction he never thought possible.

I think about what Hadley's and Jeremy's lives will be like after I'm gone. I've already picked out an urn for my ashes. Did I mention before? It's an English sugar pot from the eighteenth century in the shape of a nocturnal bird.

Wait.
I hear something
voices
shuffling
jst beyond the dorr

ggadfleyy vaREN

WES hal

HA

ha

[QUICK BLACK]

[SCENE CHANGE]

PART TWO

EX VIVO

Sotto Voce

They're all around.
And though you can't see them with your eyes,
or touch them in the usual way,
you know they are here.

You've known since you were small and sensed,
in the darkness
something not quite
still.

Like the others, but sight without looking.
Knowledge without thinking.
Feeling beyond desire or fear.
Like water, solid but also hovering.
Devoid of form, shaped by currents of life—
not still.

We begin *here* now.
A quiet room known as Sunday.
In the province of autumn,
when everything that lives is falling or
wishes to drop,
pulled home into earth's mouth,
where worms churn and whorl
the tree's damp mix,
like fortune tellers they are ringed:
know all
without knowing.

Somewhere in New Jersey
a girl gathers leaves,
counting because the impulse to organize allays fear.
Stooping, she pulls them into her arms.
Each is completely unlike the other and yet they are
indistinguishable.

The girl holds one to her face, drinks down color with
her eyes. She is puzzled by the lines embedded—by
something etched—some message that is both history
and a prediction.

When she is satisfied, the girl lets it fall a second
time from the branches of her lissome fingers with
a feeling that would break the backs of any words,
and so is destined to lodge, unsaid, where loneliness
begins and sometimes ends.

Like all children, the girl senses patterns that overlap
to give the illusion of singularity.

Like trees, she knows all, but understands little.
What she's told is the truth, is merely the safety of
division, an ignorance so perfect it's holy.

What she is certain of cannot be glimpsed all at
once, nor dragged, dying in a net of sentence.

When afternoon comes, the girl helps her mother and father rake the leaves in their garden—a summer in pieces.

Later, twilight sharpens the sky. Breath is worn in veils. The mother, father, and child put down their tools. Look at the leaves then at each other before leaping into the piles.

Laughter spreads like wings beating.

Soon, the man and woman are tired. Too much happiness brings worry.

They go in to prepare a meal that will be churned in the wet soil of their bodies, transforming one life into another, the way fire catches after being caught.

The girl remains outside in the darkness. She rakes, then jumps into the pile, then gathers up the leaves into another soft mountain to be splayed. There is no thinking; it just happens, this joy amidst the ruins.

The girl's mother watches from a window while washing things in a basin of hot water. Her hands swim in and out of sunken cups, until each vessel is pulled, glistening, through white froth like a prize. She turns from the window to a shelf of photographs. There are people there. Some sleep, while others are more alive than ever. Like the cups draining on a tea towel, absence has a practical value in how it shapes presence.

Outside, the girl is lying still in the pile—a leaf herself. The mother leans forward, taps on the window, as though trying to part the darkness, still unaware— eight years after *his* death—that what's lost is, eventually, given back. But most fail to recognize change as restoration, a perfect geometry beyond the paradox of *now*, where: a plant is not a plant, a fly is not a fly, a bird is not a bird.

Words are communal yet bring material order through spiritual separation.

The girl sits up, as if sensing a presence. The old leaves crack like tiny bones, while those still-green tongues freshly fallen can only whisper, *sotto voce*. The mother waves, but from the white rectangle of kitchen her face seems different to the girl, like the map of a place she is not old enough to visit.

The mother presses her face to the glass, as if to resist any barrier that separates.

Soon the garden drowns in its own slow music. Night unleashes terror by extinguishing the boundary between what is and what could be.

Also, stars are being lit, one by one, to illuminate a path with light both dead and living.

Soon these ancient fires will plunge soundlessly into ponds and puddles, roll and thresh atop lakes and rivers, toss in the folding seas until doused by the arrival of a curtained flame into which we shall all be born again.

But only for a day.

Another night passes, a rolling wave that never breaks.

Morning stirs in a long room of milk and pencils, paper, wax, and apples, soft and dented. There are rows of children at pale wooden desks. One gentle, sculpted face turns to the window, anesthetized by the silent fury of cloud.

Soon rain is lashing at the glass; children stir as the drops anoint all living things, equally, without requiring a single thing in return. That's why they want to play in it: rain proves the benign power of smallness.

The girl yearns to rush outside. Stomp in puddles. Feel her feet swallowed by something invisible but all around. A tension untethered. But the teacher is tapping the desk with her hand. Heads turn back to the front of the classroom—to the shadows mistaken for things themselves.

This teacher is the opposite of trees and worms: she understands everything but knows nothing. Though what she yearns to say is what she feels— that nature knowingly creates things it will inevitably lose control of, and that what appears to be chaos is just order unfurling.

The teacher is speaking now. Her words are leaves blown through a village of small houses with closed doors.

The teacher sometimes writes at home. It's quiet there with only memory clattering in the distance. And always in the same chair. Feet tucked under. A cat on her lap like a fuzzy comma. Tea cooling upward.

Unspooling dark, her pen scratches paper like a sculptor's tool, whittling excess. It is *this* person, the one who tears open words to look inside with blazing eyes and lips mute but moving, that the children want to meet. It is *this* person they can learn from. They sense her, of course; it is the only reason they listen now, out of sympathy for the prisoner.

Outside, the sky is a bruise torn open.

Rain breaks up the day, divides it into pieces small enough for a pocket, the back of a hand, the fabric of a shoe, a splinter of eyelash.

And here is the father in between patients:
Polished shoes round and black as a dog's nose.
One hand holds a telephone while the other writes.

And here is the girl's mother, driving. A blue car now with a roof that opens and a back seat of unread magazines. A silk scarf is tied about her neck. A deep, soft green made by worms. It's all that remains of them; a sacrifice not kind, but instinctual. The father gave the scarf to the mother for a birthday. She remembers the box: bright orange but pebbled to the touch.
There was perfume, too, spring in a bottle.

It was not the value of the gift so much as the effort to procure it that made her feel safe.

Her fingers pull sideways on the steering wheel as one foot pushes just enough. Tires on the wet road like faint ripping. Headlights fill each falling drop with gold.

The woman will soon be at the place she works, walking between desks toward her desk trailing fragrance like loose ribbon.

Now the girl Maxine is outside.

It's recess and she moves over a grassy field with Doris, her best friend. The ground is drenched. Splinters of green stick to the toes of their shoes.

"Yesterday I raked all the leaves. Then guess what, Doris?"

"What?"

"Mummy and daddy and me jumped in them and then I had to rake them all again, BY MYSELF."

Doris's eyes move around but settle on nothing, actual sight diverted by imagination.

"There were leaves everywhere!" exclaims Maxine, now spreading the wings of her arms.

A passing boy stops, panting like a small dog. He turns to Maxine and Doris. His shoes and socks are drenched from the wet field.

"Did you see any animals in the leaves?" he asks.

The girls look at one another, then back at the boy.

"Sometimes animals live in the piles, you know," he goes on.

"Yes, Gareth—raccoons do," Doris informs him.

"I didn't see any of those," Maxine admits, "but there's an owl that lives in my tree."

The boy's hot cheeks redden. "Did you see it?"

Maxine glances upward through branches of memory, all the way to imagination. "No, because he was sleeping."

"In the tree?" asks Doris.

Maxine nods. "Hmm. It's his home. Way above the garden in a tree hole."

"Can he touch the moon?" asks the boy. "Grab it like a cookie?"

"He drinks from the moon every night, actually," says Maxine. "It's where owl milk comes from."

"Milk comes from cows," says the boy. "Except chocolate milk, which is from a factory."

"Well, I think all milk comes from the moon," admits Doris.

"So . . . then what are cows?" asks the boy, blinking quickly.

"They're *aminals* Gareth," says Doris, "that stand around in fields looking at each other going *moooooooooOOOOOOOOooooooo.*"

They all do it.

They all go, *mooooooOOOOooooOOOOOOOO oooOOOOOOOoooo* until bells clang over the field like ropes, pulling them in for lunch.

The clouds swim higher and drift as one.

Those who die are the same ones being born.

A ring of days is forged by night.

The world around begins to harden as autumn grits its teeth.

The morning air is sharp; everything green is brittled by frost.

Maxine darts about a large hall with a wooden floor. There is deep breathing and the *scootch* of rubber shoes as soft legs turn and balls bounce madly between grasping hands.

"That's it! Now hold your balls! Good, Gareth! Good, Maxine! Doris, where's your ball?"

Jeremy, the father, is at work. There is the writing of numbers, and the writing of sentences. Dosing and deliberation. The goal is a common goal. Beyond that, nobody really knows. Then a fizz from his pocket. It's his wife, her name and photograph pulse on the screen as he taps a button to release her voice.

"Jeremy?"

"Everything okay, darling?"

"Are you busy?"

"No, I've got four hours until my next patient. What's up?"

"I'm not feeling well."

"Oh no. Maybe you picked up the sniffles from Maxine?"

"No, not like that."

"Oh . . ."

"I didn't know who else to call. Sorry."

"Don't be sorry. It's why I'm here. It's part of being your husband."

"It's not something I can control."

"Look, it's lunchtime. Why don't I leave the office and pick you up in a half hour?"

"No, it's okay. I'm okay. I just wanted to hear your voice."

"Did something happen?"

"No."

"Just a feeling, huh?"

"Today is his birthday."

Jeremy senses something small and hot, a meteor blazing words. But he says nothing, lets the moment cool to rock, then fall where he will never find it.

"How old would he have been?"

"It doesn't matter . . ."

The sound of her breathing fills the space between them. Language is a map leading to a place not on the map.

"Why don't I come and get you?" he says. "We could have lunch at the Lotos Club or go play a few games of tennis, maybe you'll even let me win one."

"I'm okay."

"You don't sound okay."

"I think I just needed to tell someone."

"I should have remembered."

"No, it's not like I remember your mother's birthday. I'm just so sorry to put you through this, over and over," she says. "I mean, it's been eight years for god's sake."

Loving the dead is like moss growing on stone.

"Oh, I don't mind, honey. Remember that all my happiness is because of him."

The woman feels her heart ripping, but only to reveal a new one, which in turn must be torn up.

"Think of us as a team," he tells her. "The four of us on a mission."

She blows her nose, even laughs a little. "But what's the mission?"

"Well, that's the exciting part, isn't it?"

"Exciting is *one* way to put it, I suppose."

Jeremy is silent. Old enough now to know their story is common, and that unyielding pain is preferable to the agony of nothing.

After lunch, outside on the playground, children stand in clusters like flickering stars of flesh, bone, hair, and breathing.

"What are you going to be for Halloween?" asks Gareth. "I'm an owl like the one in your tree, Maxine."

Maxine knits the boy's words as her body softens with feathers and her face rounds into something white with eyes like cave pools. It's windy where she watches from a finger of night, the child, the mother, the father, others too, she sees, silvered by moonlight in sleep.

Then Doris screams, "I'm going to be a fox, which means I live alone and eat mice by the dozen!"

"I thought you loved mice," says Maxine, thoughtfully.

"No," says Doris. "That's bats."

"But a bat *is* a mouse that can fly."

"Well," muses Doris, "I eat those, too . . . when I feel like it."

"I can see in the dark," says Maxine. "So, you can't eat me. I'm too quick."

Gareth steps closer. "You're not an owl, are you? Maxine, that's what I'm being."

"I am a rabbit like I was before. It's a simple life, sniffing grass and eating carrots for every meal, even snack."

"Oh good," says Doris. "I might have to eat you up, too. I like a good rabbit."

Maxine feels their laughter as small, soft blows. But then her ears stretch. Back legs clench and recoil. "You have to catch me first!" She bolts. The owl and the fox move quickly without thinking.

Teeth are visible. Claws rip the ground as small shoes go clopping and clapping hands mean flight.

Little feet have given way to paws and feathered wings. The scream and shriek and growl and terror and ecstasy of children untangling.

The curtain of night is falling
and things felt in the day
pain and joy alike
are being disassembled
in order to be built again
tomorrow.

Maxine runs from her mother's car to the front door, then turns back and watches the woman who was born when she was born gather things from the back seat of her blue car and approach with the glistening house key held aloft. The lock swallows, and the door swings to reveal the familiar, comforting stomach of home.

Inside, Hadley walks around the house and snaps on lights, considering what to cook.

Maxine stands in one place and takes off her coat, lets it drop. Her mother calls to her from the kitchen amidst the clamor of pans and pots pulled from cupboards.

"Did you learn anything interesting today?"

Maxine answers but forgets to speak.

"Well?" says her mother. "I hope you're not talking to Doris during the lessons."

"Doris is not my best friend anymore."

"What happened?"

"She became a fox and put a worm in my schoolbag."

"Why?"

"An owl told her to."

"Are you listening to your teacher?"

"I'm always listening."

"Good. That's what you're there for, sweetheart."

Maxine lingers in the doorway, between rooms,

sniffing the air as it fills with the aroma of onions crackling in the big pan.

"Can I go outside?"

"Come in here, please, Maxine . . . I'm making supper and can't hear you."

"I said, can I go outside?"

"Outside? But it's dark, sweetheart."

"I know. But I have to find someone."

"Who?"

"Owl."

"What owl?"

"The one who lives in the tree hole."

"In the garden? Who told you that?"

"I need to get an owl feather."

"An owl feather. Why?"

"For Halloween. I promised Gareth."

"Did you decide on a Halloween costume? Why don't you do that instead of wandering around outside? We only have a couple of days if you want me to make your costume."

"I'm going to be a rabbit."

"You were a rabbit last year."

Maxine shrugs. "I guess that means I love rabbits."

"What about a ghost?" asks Hadley.

"No thanks. I'm a rabbit girl."

"You don't want to be something scary? Like a zombie? It is Halloween, after all."

"What's a zombie again?"

"A person who won't die . . . who keeps coming back no matter what."

Maxine looks at her fingers. "Why is that scary?"

"I suppose . . ." says her mother, dropping the utensil, "because they walk like this . . ."

Maxine laughs to please her mother, who is trying to please her. "That's not scary," she says.

"Ooh, how about a ghost rabbit? That's frightening!"

"Not to me, it's not." But then Maxine imagines the glowing outline of a creature not quite there. "*Can* animals be ghosts, Mom?"

"I don't see why not."

Maxine thinks for a moment. "Have you ever met a ghost?"

Hadley's face changes. Like a mechanical toy, she turns to the wall where photographs hang, suspended over the past. There is one that sits apart from the others.

In the distance, memories circle like birds ready to land—if she'll let them.

Maxine follows her mother's eyes. "Who is that again, Mom?

"A friend."

"Your friend who died?"

"Yes. I told you . . . he was my husband once."

"Before Daddy?"

"Yes."

"Did you have a baby with him?"

Hadley marvels at how quickly the eyes of pain flash open.

"What was his name?"

"Who?"

"Your husband before Daddy."

"His name was Max."

"Like me."

"You were named after him, actually. It was Daddy's idea."

"So, I can't meet him?"

"No, my darling, he died."

"Why?"

"He had a rare disease."

"How did he get it?"

"I don't know."

"Could Daddy get it, too?"

"Yes . . . but he won't."

"How come?"

"I don't know. He just won't."

For Maxine, so many sentences lead to confusion, as though she is arriving in many places at once.

"He died before you were born, Maxine."

"Was he friends with Daddy, too?"

"Oh yes. I met Daddy *because* of Max."

The child nods, piecing together the puzzle of her mother's words.

"Then is Max a ghost now?"

"What?"

"Maybe I could be him for Halloween?"

Hadley stares at her daughter as if some part of her is only now finding out. All she can do is go back to making dinner—or a part of her can, as there are many versions inside the one that is visible.

Maxine is left alone with faces that made her life possible.

"So, can I go outside and look for him?" she asks without realizing.

When Jeremy gets home, he hovers over the steaming pots as Hadley tells him what happened. The sting has gone, leaving only a small bump. He kisses the top of her head, then removes three water glasses from the cupboard.

After dinner, the house is quiet.

In her room, Maxine shifts things in a dollhouse, little wooden pieces once hidden in trees, now tiny versions of the girl. Her hands move deliberately as she talks for the dolls, helps them understand how it feels to feel.

Jeremy is folding laundry from the dryer, while downstairs, Hadley rinses plates and cups.

Eight years ... she thinks ... Eight times around the sun ...

And now the time ahead like open fields to be crossed.

Then something moves out in the garden, Hadley inhales and grips the sink edge with both hands. Leaning forward, she strains, but sees only her reflection skating upon the glass.

She opens the back door.

Cold pours in—but out she goes, stepping carefully onto night's first page.

She walks to the place where she saw it moving from the window. Stands there herself, waiting to feel something.

Then Jeremy is in the open door.

"Everything alright?"

"I thought I saw something."

"What?"

"I don't know ... like the flash of something."

Jeremy steps out in his socks. Moves toward his

wife. The ground is still wet. Hadley is about to speak when she notices on the path between them, a white glow—more a gesture of something than the thing itself.

Hadley stoops to collect a feather, then presses the silken overture of flight to her cheek, as if to prove it's there.

Slowly, she glances up to where the tree ends and night begins.

But everything that is not darkness

must be imagined

ACKNOWLEDGMENTS

The author wishes to express his gratitude and admiration for the greatest editor in publishing, Joshua Bodwell. Praise also must go to Tammy Ackerman and Milan Bozic for design excellence, Godine publisher David Allender for his support, Elizabeth Blachman for her x-ray vision as copy editor, Celia Johnson and Madeleine Van Booy for their close scrutiny as proofreaders, and to literary agent Susanna Lea, along with her team, Kerry Glencorse, Noa Rosen, and Helena Sandlying-Jacobsen.

The author would also like to point out that in chapter twelve there is an observation about language that seems too close to Jacques Derrida's notion of *différance* to withhold acknowledgment. And in chapter eight, Carol's line of dialogue about the suffering of others appears to be a concept explored by C. S. Lewis in his book *God in the Dock: Essays on Theology and Ethics.*

A NOTE ABOUT THE AUTHOR

Simon Van Booy is the award-winning, bestselling author of more than a dozen books for adults and children. He is the editor of three volumes of philosophy and has written for the *New York Times*, *Financial Times*, *Washington Post*, and the BBC. Raised in rural North Wales, he currently lives in New York where he is also a book editor and a volunteer EMT for Central Park Medical Unit and Ridgewood Volunteer Ambulance Corps.

A NOTE ON THE TYPE

The Presence of Absence has been set in Aldus. Designed by Hermann Zapf and released by the German type foundry Stempel in 1954, Aldus is lighter and more refined than its family member Palatino, which is perhaps Zapf's most famous design. The popularity of Palatino after its release in 1949 led to its use in the body text of books, something Zapf had never intended for the display face. The elegant Aldus was his solution for book designers enamored with Palatino.

Design & Composition by Tammy Ackerman